Ellen A Proctor

A brief Memoir of Christina G. Rossetti

Ellen A Proctor

A brief Memoir of Christina G. Rossetti

ISBN/EAN: 9783743349513

Manufactured in Europe, USA, Canada, Australia, Japa

Cover: Foto ©Andreas Hilbeck / pixelio.de

Manufactured and distributed by brebook publishing software
(www.brebook.com)

Ellen A Proctor

A brief Memoir of Christina G. Rossetti

PORTRAIT OF MISS ROSSETTI,

Taken from that in " The Girlhood of the Blessed Virgin," by D. G. Rossetti.

A BRIEF MEMOIR

OF

Christina G. Rossetti.

BY

ELLEN A. PROCTOR.

WITH A PREFACE BY

W. M. ROSSETTI.

S.P.C.K.,

LONDON: NORTHUMBERLAND AVENUE, W.C.

1895.

[PUBLISHED UNDER THE DIRECTION OF
THE TRACT COMMITTEE.]

PREFATORY NOTE.

VERY soon after the death of my beloved sister Christina, on December 29, 1894, I learned that Miss Proctor was disposed to write something concerning her. I encouraged her to do so, being well aware that my sister had entertained a very cordial feeling towards her, had seen a good deal of

her from time to time, and
had up to the very last been
in communication with her,
either personally or by correspondence. Indeed, I had
more than once, during the
closing two or three months
of Christina's life, opened
some letter addressed to her
by Miss Proctor, and had
read it aloud to her—for she
was then much too far gone
to open or read letters for
herself, or of course to reply
to them. The following pages,
written by Miss Proctor in
fulfilment of her intention,

8

have been carefully perused by me. I find them to present a pleasant and interesting little portrait of my sister, and a true one; for the traits of character indicated by Miss Proctor are such as I was myself highly familiar with. They marked my sister throughout her life of sixty-four years, and more especially in its closing decade.

WM. M. ROSSETTI.

LONDON,
July, 1895.

A Brief Memoir of Christina G. Rossetti.

ALTHOUGH much popular en-
thusiasm has been lately called
forth by the writings of the late
Miss Christina Rossetti, and
the nation's regret has found
sympathetic expression at her
lamented death, a supple-
mentary tribute to her saintly

life may not be without interest to all who value the religious character of her works.

For nearly fifteen years I have enjoyed the privilege of her friendship, counsel, sympathy, and of that love for others which was the keynote of her life, and showed itself undiminished even in her illness and suffering. One of her last sentences was, " I love everybody. If ever I had an enemy, I should hope to meet and welcome that enemy to heaven."

Christina Georgina Rossetti was born on December 5, 1830, in Charlotte Street, Portland Place, London, and died on December 29, 1894, at 30, Torrington Square, W.C., aged sixty-four. She was the youngest child of Gabriel Rossetti, an Italian poet of high repute in his native country, who, however, was obliged, from political troubles, to take up his abode here. In England he is best known as a commentator on Dante. Some time after his arrival he married Frances Polidori, who was born in England, but of Italian extraction. Her father, Gaetano Polidori, was well known as a translator of Milton into Italian. Her brother was the physician who accompanied Lord Byron to the Continent in the year 1816. The other children of this union were Maria Francesca, the author of a "Shadow of Dante," and other works. This lady entered the sisterhood of "All Saints," and died in 1876, three years later. Her loss was deeply felt by Christina, who had previously expressed her sisterly feeling thus—

> "There is no friend like a sister in
>   calm or stormy weather,
> To cheer one on the tedious way,
> To fetch one if one goes astray,
> To lift one if one totters down,
> To strengthen whilst one stands."

Her elder brother, Dante Gabriel Rossetti, was born in 1828, and died 1882. His fame as a poet and artist is well known. It is enough to say that he was one of the founders of the English pre-Raphaelites, and that his paintings, "Beata Beatrix" and the "Annunciation," are now in the National Gallery. For the latter his sister Christina was the model, as, indeed, she was for a still earlier painting, "The Girlhood of Mary Virgin," and it is gratifying to know that her features will be remembered, as her writings are sure to be.

Her younger brother, William Michael Rossetti, is now the last survivor of the family; he it was who tenderly devoted himself to and comforted her in her last illness, and, with his young family, her only other relatives, saw the last sad duties performed. She sleeps with her mother in Highgate Cemetery, not far from what she called her "world of brick and mortar," where for many years she thought and wrote and prayed so much.

Mr. William Michael Rossetti is well known as a poet and critic, and as having edited Shelley. His published poems make us regret that one who can write so well has not written more.

Christina Rossetti was entirely educated at home under

the supervision of her highly accomplished and intellectual mother, whose sterling character and strong religious principles influenced her childish years. As the constant companion of her brothers, it may not be wrong to say that she acquired an independence of thought and feeling which, with an ordinary English education, she could scarcely have attained. Hers was a delightfully happy home: love, poetry, art, religion,—everything that could make life sweet. Of her mother she writes in dedicating her poems to her, "To my mother, to whom I inscribe my book in all reverence and love;" and again—

"To my first love, my mother,
On whose knee I learnt love-lore
that is not troublesome,
Whose service is my special
dignity,
And she my lode-star."

The brothers and sisters read very much, and almost the same books. Italian they knew perfectly, and their father's poems influenced their early notions and habits of mind. When but ten years old, Christina read the operatic poems of Metastasio in Italian, which contain many graceful lyrics. She read and admired Shakespeare at a very early age, as did her brothers — " Hamlet " being a favourite play. Scott, Byron, and to some extent Burns, were read in turns. Pope's " Iliad " was an especial favourite, and at the age of eleven Dante Gabriel made a series of pen-and-ink illustrations for it. Ariosto's " Orlando Furioso " was read by the brothers in the original. Goethe's " Faust," Carleton's

"Traits and Stories of the Irish Peasantry," Miss Edgeworth's stories, and Peter Parley's books were much appreciated. In addition, the "Arabian Nights," "Robinson Crusoe," "The Ballad of Chevy Chase," even "Jack the Giant Killer," had been read by the family with great interest in their youthful days.

Scriptural lore was not forgotten, and the Rossettis were well versed in this at an early age.

Christina Rossetti's first poem, on her mother's birthday,

was written in 1842, when
she was but eleven years old.
It ran thus—

TO MY MOTHER.

WITH A NOSEGAY.

"To-day's your natal day,
    Sweet flowers I bring:
Mother, accept, I pray,
    My offering.

"And may you happy live,
    And long us bless;
Receiving as you give
    Great happiness."

This, and many other poems
also written at a very early
age, were privately printed by
her grandfather Polidori, and

are marvellous productions for one so young. Even at this time a religious element strongly pervades the series.

In January, 1850, a periodical called the *Germ* (or, *Thoughts towards Nature in Poetry, Literature, and Art*) first appeared. This was a monthly journal, at the head of which were the brothers Rossetti. Holman Hunt, Woolner, and others contributed.

Christina Rossetti, who wrote under the *nom de plume* of Ellen Alleyne, was herself a contributor. One of her

most characteristic poems,
called "Dream-Land," ap-
peared in the first number of
the *Germ*, January, 1850.

"Where sunless rivers weep
  Their waves into the deep,
  She sleeps a charmèd sleep:
    Awake her not.
  Led by a single star,
  She came from very far,
  To seek where shadows are,
    Her pleasant lot.

"She left the rosy morn,
  She left the fields of corn,
  For twilight cold and torn,
    And water-springs.
  Thro' sleep as thro' a veil,
  She sees the sky look pale,
  And hears the nightingale
    That sadly sings.

24

"Rest, rest, a perfect rest,
  Shed over brow and breast;
  Her face is toward the west,
    The purple land.
  She cannot see the grain
  Ripening on hill and plain,
  She cannot feel the rain
    Upon her hand.

" Rest, rest for evermore,
  Upon a mossy shore;
  Rest to the heart's core,
    Till time shall cease.
  Sleep that no pain shall wake,
  Night that no morn shall break,
  Till joy shall overtake
    Her perfect peace."

"A Pause of Thought"
and a " Testimony," from the
pen of Eilen Alleyne, appeared
the following month, February,

1850. During the continuance of the periodical she contributed regularly to it. This was her first essay in public writing. In the February number of this publication the "Blessed Damozel" of her elder brother appeared—a creation he afterwards embodied on canvas. The tender beauty of this poem alone would have made his fame. The "Cordelia" of Mr. William M. Rossetti followed.

The first collection of Miss Rossetti's poems, bearing her own name, and entitled

"Goblin Market, and other Poems," was printed in 1862. This volume, containing as it does some of her most charming lyrics, became speedily popular.

The grotesque, uncanny figures conjured up in "Goblin Market" struck the public fancy, and the fame of the young poetess was at once established.

Many of her songs are mournfully sweet, as the following :—

"Come to me in the silence of the
    night,
Come in the speaking silence of a
    dream ;

Come with soft rounded cheeks,
and eyes as bright
As sunlight on a stream ;
Come back in tears,
O memory, hope, love of finished
years !

"Oh ! dream how sweet, too sweet,
too bitter sweet,
Whose waking should have been
in Paradise,
Where souls brimful of love abide
and meet,
Where thirsty longing eyes
Watch the slow door,
That opening, letting in, lets out
no more !

"Yet come to me in dreams, that
I may live
My very life again, though cold
in death !

28

Come back to me in dreams, that
    I may give
Pulse for pulse, breath for
    breath :
    Speak low, lean low,
As long ago, my love, how long
    ago ! "

About a year before her
death I was visiting Miss
Rossetti. We talked of poetry
and various authors, alluding
to the poem I have just
quoted. I asked her if she
knew the author of the following lines :—

"Oh ! love, I am unblest,
  With monstrous doubts opprest,
Of much that's dark and nether !

Much that's holiest and best,—
Could I but win you for an hour
from off that starry shore,
The hunger of my soul were stilled;
For Death has told you more
Than the melancholy world doth
know,
Things beyond all lore."

She was very much struck
with the lines, and said, "I
felt like that once; now I
trust and submit."

But to stop digression: that
she had attained a stage beyond the hopeless yearning
for the loved and lost, is
marked in her poem en-
titled "Up Hill."

30

"Does the road wind uphill all
the way?
Yes, to the very end.
Will the day's journey take the
whole long day?
From morn to night, my friend.

"But is there for the night a resting-
place?
A roof for when the slow dark
hours begin?
May not the darkness hide it from
my face?
You cannot miss that inn.

"Shall I meet other wayfarers at
night?
Those who have gone before.
Then must I knock, or call when
just in sight?
They will not keep you standing
at that door.

"Shall I find comfort, travel-sore
   and weak?
   Of labour you shall find the
   sum.
   Will there be beds for me and all
   who seek?
   Yea, beds for all who come."

At the close of her book
are devotional pieces, and at
the end of an old-year ditty
she concludes with—

"Watch with me, Jesus, in my
   loneliness;
   Though others say me nay, yet
   say Thou yes;
   Though others pass me by, stop
   Thou to bless!
   Yea, Thou dost stop with me
   this vigil night;

To-night of pain, to-morrow of
delight.
I, Love, am Thine; Thou, Lord
my God, art mine."

In 1866 Miss Rossetti published "The Prince's Pro-
gress, and other Poems." In
1870, a volume named "Com-
monplace, and other Short
Stories." Two years later,
"Sing-Song," a nursery-rhyme
book which any child can
enjoy. The same may be
said of "Speaking Likenesses,"
published in 1874—both vol-
umes being illustrated. A
contrast to the latter also

appeared in 1874, "Annus Domini," a volume of prayers for each day in the year. In 1879, "Short Studies of the Benedicite," and "Seek and Find," both prose works. "Called to be Saints," a volume in which the Minor Festivals are devotionally studied, was published the following year, and dedicated, in hope of reunion, to the dear and gracious memory of her sister. In 1881, "A Pageant, and other Poems" was published; "Letter and Spirit," or Notes on the Commandments, 1883; and shortly after, "Time Flies," a diary in prose and verse. A commentary on the Revelation was next published, entitled "The Face of the Deep." This was dedicated "To my mother, for the first time to her beloved, revered, cherished memory," and published in 1892.

Miss Rossetti's position as one of the first poets of the nineteenth century being fully established, criticism on her works, which have been so ably reviewed, would be valueless.

The *Century Magazine* for 1894 describes her as the most perfect of the contemporary poets. The Right Hon. W. E. Gladstone has expressed the same opinion. Her sonnets are perfect in form, and it has been said the influence of Dante may be seen in the perfection of finish of her most playful and even fantastic work.

This is noticeable even in her childish work, privately printed; for instance, "Lady Isabella" and "Vanity of Vanities," sonnets which are

perfect, containing two sets of
four quatrains and two sets
of three terzettes, with the
leading thought well sustained
throughout. This could not
have been said always, even
of the company of "courtly
makers" of the Elizabethan
age, Wyatt excepted.

The "Prince's Progress"
is a poem which, once read,
creates a desire to read over
again and again. It might
be called a Tennysonian
poem; it haunts the brain and
the memory, and is a perfect
piece of word-painting; as—

"What is this that comes through
    the door,
The face covered the feet before?

.   .   .   .   .

  Veiled figures carrying her
  Sweep by, yet make no stir;
A bride-chant burdened with one
    name;
  The bride-song rises steadier
  Than the torches' flame."

Her maidens chide the dila-
tory prince with—

"Is she fair now as she lies?
  Once she was fair;
Meet queen for any kingly king,
  With gold-dust on her hair;
Now these are poppies in her
    locks,
  White poppies she must wear.

  .   .   .   .

38

"You should have wept her yester-
    day,
  Wasting upon her bed.

    .   .   .   .   .

  Lo, we who love weep not to-
    day,
  But crown her royal head.
  Let be these poppies that we
    strew ;
  Your roses are too red."

Christina Rossetti's poems
are not all of this dirge-like
character. "Maiden - Song"
terminates with the marriages
of three sisters. "Goblin
Market" finishes in like character; and what more joyful
pæan can be found than "The
Birthday"?—

" My heart is like a singing-bird,
   Whose nest is in a watered
     shoot ;
My heart is like an apple tree,
   Whose boughs are bent with
     thick-set fruit ;
My heart is like a rainbow shell,
   'That paddles in a halcyon
     sea ;
My heart is gladder than all
    these,
   Because my love is come to
    me.

• "Raise me a daïs of silk and
    down,
   Hang it with vair and purple
    dyes ;
Carve it in doves and pome-
    granates,
   And peacocks with a hundred
    eyes ;

Work it in gold and silver grapes,
In leaves and silver fleurs-de-
lys;
Because the birthday of my life
Is come, my love is come to
me."

Here the imagery seems partly
suggested by the Song of
Solomon.

My acquaintance with Miss
Rossetti commenced in this
wise. We met at the house of
a mutual friend, Miss C——,
a lady well known in Blooms-
bury and at St. Giles's Poor-
house for her good works.
A group of ladies assembled

at afternoon tea were talking
on various subjects. It was
somehow mentioned that I
had recently returned from
the Cape, and different ques-
tions about the country were
asked me. One lady near
me seemed much interested.
The conversation turned on
the Zulu war and its dis-
asters, and the ill-fated 24th
Regiment. I was eloquent on
this subject. I had known
many of the killed at Isan-
dula, and had even been
taken to supper by Melville
at their last ball, given by

Lady Frere in Cape Town. When I described the dash made for the Queen's colours by the two friends, Coghill and Melville, this lady said, "It sounds like the knights of old doing battle for a lady's favour." I believe I quoted the lines of Sir Francis Doyle—

"And now, forgetting that wild ride, forgetful of all pain,
High amongst those who have not lived, who have not died, in vain,
By strange stars watched, they sleep afar."

At length I began to remember that I was talking

rather long and exclusively to this one lady with the eloquent speaking eyes, and changed the subject. In a short time some others rose to leave, and one said, "Goodbye, Miss Rossetti." I turned to my late companion, and said, "Are you Miss Rossetti?" "Yes," she said cheerily, "I am." "Miss Christina Rossetti?" I continued. "Christina Rossetti, at your service!" was the reply. She was smiling now, and her face seemed to say, "What a wonder you make of me!" And I repeated, "Did you really write that beautiful hymn, 'Good Friday'?" "Yes," she said slowly, "I did." And her face at once became grave and solemn. I may here transcribe the poem—

"Am I a stone, and not a sheep,
That I can stand, O Christ, beneath
      Thy cross,
To number drop by drop Thy
      Blood's slow loss,
      And yet not weep?

" Not so those women loved,
Who with exceeding grief lamented
      Thee;
Not so fallen Peter weeping bitterly;
      Not so the thief was moved;

"Not so the sun and moon,
Which hid their faces in a starless
  sky,
A horror of great darkness at broad
  noon ;—
  I, only I.

" Yet give not o'er,
But seek Thy sheep, true Shepherd
  of the flock.
Greater than Moses, turn and look
  once more,
  And smite a rock."

This it was that cemented
our friendship, the sympathy
in Christ's suffering ; and no
stronger bond could be found
for her, none could touch the
core of her heart like that,
Thus years rolled on; we met

46

often, and I was always received as a welcome guest. I
left the country again for some
years, during which time we
regularly corresponded. It was
during my absence her fatal
illness commenced. She did
not like to distress me with the
knowledge of what that illness
was. She had undergone a
serious operation, and wrote
to me from Brighton—

"Your letter arrived when
I was too ill to attend to
correspondence; now I have
rallied considerably. My good
old aunt [Miss Polidori] keeps

fairly well, and I am happy to find that my daily letter to her since I came here has amused her. Good accounts of her have followed me hither, and to-morrow I hope to resume my post in her room."

Always self-sacrificing and ready to devote herself to others, yet she writes that it was full five years since she had left London before, and that the change had been "truly reviving and refreshing." When often urged to have a change to the country, her reply was, "Not on any account would I leave my aunt for a day, even ; my duty lies here. One day, perhaps, when I am left alone, I shall see the country again." In one of her poems she says—

> " Why, one day in the country
> Is worth a month in town ;
> Is worth a day and a year."

She sometimes said, " When my aunt leaves me, should I survive her, I should like to live in Kent, near Rochester, if possible." That wish was never to be realized. Although, after her aunt's death, she had quite decided on leaving

London, her malady increased so rapidly that her departure was found to be impracticable. Miss Rossetti was a devout member of the English Church, as she says herself, "The beloved Anglican Church of my baptism." Her former clergyman, Rev. H. W. Burrows, had become a Canon of Rochester Cathedral; hence her desire to live near it.

At the close of 1890 a break occurred in the monotony of her life, and she wrote to me at the Cape: "I have just lately been having my brother and his family (six in number) staying here, as they were changing their abode. This made a great change and stir up in my quiet habits; and as they all seemed very comfortable in their temporary quarters, I was comfortable too."

During my stay at the Cape, and referring to my home in Wynberg, she wrote, "What a lovely picture—a garden full of arums!" And again, "I wonder what blue plumbago is like? Perhaps I may have seen, but I do not identify it.

Surely it is not to be despised at your window, though it may not vie with primroses? * As I no longer go to the country from time to time, I may say the country very graciously comes to me, for friends send or bring me flowers."

About this time the failure

* I should have mentioned that blue plumbago is the pride of Wynberg, where all the hedges are composed of it; that is, when they are not of blue myrtle. When left to Nature, sheets of pale blue flowers enchant all beholders. There are, however, many Vandals who keep such carefully clipped.

of the Cape of Good Hope Bank, following after another, caused widespread distress.

Miss Rossetti wrote, "I have seen the bank failure announced in the paper, and am sorry for all whom it involves in ruin or distress; even to a wealthy person £3500 is a serious loss. Poor Miss ——! Really it is sometimes a comfort not to possess a fortune, so that one cannot lose it."

At Christmas she wrote, "I do not know how long a letter takes on its way to the

Cape; but this is intended to wish you every blessing of Christmas, and of 1892. We twain are much as of yore, my poor old aunt still lingering on without (most mercifully) any very great apparent suffering."

Of Ireland she writes in 1888, "I trust your stay in Ireland promoted your health as well as spirits. I used to think I should like to see something of that near-at-hand island; but, then, I do not particularly fancy the rough passage, not to hint at the

alienated section of the nation !
So, apparently, I am as well,
or better, at home, which is
convenient. As to recovery,
my aunt's state is hopeless;
yet I know not at all how long
her gradual decay may last.
Very mercifully she is spared
much pain."

In a later letter she said,
" I am not well, nor do I look
forward to ever being very
strong again." This was
alarming. I returned from the
Cape in 1892, and found
matters much worse than
I had supposed. She had

undergone an operation for cancer, and her heart's action was also seriously affected. No one, however, ever heard her complain or murmur. She always received me with cheerfulness, which only gave way to sadness when listening to any tale of woe concerning others. I have frequently seen tears in her eyes on such occasions.

During my stay in Dorsetshire she wrote constantly. In one letter she says—

"What a haven of rest a country rectory must be! I do not know your part of the world, but doubt not it includes features I should admire; amongst others, Purbeck marble, which I recall to memory. When I was in Devonshire (once only, at Torquay), I was much struck with the varied beauty of the Devon marbles."

Here Miss Rossetti was confounding Dorsetshire with Devon; she would have been still more struck with the beauty of the Isle of Purbeck, with Swanage and its lovely bay, whose perfect curve delights the painter.

Her last surviving aunt, Miss Polidori, died in June, 1893, so that practically her cares were over. On the day of Miss Polidori's funeral I sat for some hours with her. "I hope to retain her good nurse for myself," she said. "I shall require her services, for, humanly speaking, my malady does not admit of a cure." I may here mention that the nurse, Miss Read, remained with her to the last, and was a great comfort, and most devoted to her patient. Miss Read accompanied Miss

Rossetti to Brighton in August, 1893, for a few months' visit. At this time I lost an aunt, and went over to Ireland to settle up her affairs. From Brighton she wrote, " This is such a quiet life that we are leading, it supplies but little matter for letters. Sometimes I go out in a chair, now and then in a fly, pretty often for a short walk, very short ; but I am obviously better, and who knows what another fortnight may effect ? " She did return to London considerably better, and I also came back from Ireland in November, greatly harassed by my land difficulties. Miss Rossetti was the sympathizing friend, who was ready to condole with, and give help and counsel in all emergencies.

I returned to the Isle of Saints at Christmas, 1893, and she wrote, " What a complication of anxious trouble ! You far exceed me in spirit; but what I should do in your place I know not. I look forward to hearing from you again, and shall want to know how matters went on the 23rd,

but of course I can fully under-
stand how busy and occupied
you may be, and I beg you
not to write till convenient
and agreeable to yourself."

I had at this time to serve
three ejectments before I
could gain possession of my
late aunt's house or lands.
Having succeeded with all
three, she wrote, "I con-
gratulate you heartily on this
success after a long strain
of anxiety." The success,
however, was temporary and
short-lived.

I regret that at this time

I was much occupied with my own affairs, and I fear more a trouble than a comfort to my friend, who was always cheerful herself, and took the brightest side of things. Yet she condescended to notice ordinary events. In one letter she writes, "My cat has presented us with a kitten, for which we have found a home, so the nice little thing is being reared."

The faithful "Muff"—the cat here mentioned—was a great favourite, and has now found comfortable quarters in the home of Mr. W. M. Rossetti. Of her may be said—

"A Poet's cat, sedate and grave,
As Poet well might wish to have."

On August 29, 1893, Miss Rossetti wrote from Brighton to Ireland: "I am very glad you have safely performed your journey to Rathcoursey, and received two hearty welcomes. May more follow! No wonder you were driven back by the heat when you kindly set off to see me. Nurse and I came hither on that most broiling day, Wednesday the 16th, and I feel all the better for this complete change. All favouring, I propose to remain here four weeks, thus going home on the 13th. I am glad your cats find friends. Our poor Muff, it seems, missed us at first, but has since recovered her equanimity."

In 1893, Miss Rossetti wrote of her last Christmas but one, "My Christmas Day was very quiet; I could not go to church, and saw no one but my small household. For the first time on that day I saw my nurse in your pretty Madeira apron. Most of the other fine pieces of needlework I gave to my sister-in-law, who duly admired them, I trust. I must thank you for the pleasure which I had in giving them away " — alluding to some work I had brought from Madeira.

She had the deepest sympathy with the sufferings of the poor, and thus expresses it in January, 1894—

" The weather here has been exceptionally rigorous,

but now that is over, and comfort revives. Distress is, indeed, widespread—so much so that your young woman" (alluding to a young Irish widow I was interested in), "who goes four miles for food and sixpence, becomes enviable. The contrast between London luxury and London destitution is really appalling. All sorts of gaieties advertised, and deaths by exposure or starvation recorded in the same newspaper."

In 1886 and 1887 I was engaged in parish work in

Ratcliff. My mission was to go on Monday nights to the Factory Girls' Club, London Street, under the special care of the vicar, Rev. R. K. Arbuthnot. Here congregated many of Bryant and May's workers, but rope-makers, satchel - makers, jam - makers, and all the industries of the East End were represented. Many were of Irish parentage and Roman Catholics. The object was to try and interest them in something, and get them into the club after work was over. Miss

Rossetti took a deep interest in the welfare of these young people, and would herself have liked to become a working member of the club, had her nursing duties allowed it; but at that time she had two aunts, quite invalids, to tend.

In returning home, which I never did before eleven o'clock p.m., many incidents struck me on the route. I was accustomed to relate all to Miss Rossetti, who specially wished to hear how the evening had been passed. At one time it was the tiny children returning home alone, their part being over at the Theatre, that excited her commiseration, and she said—

"London makes mirth, but I know
God hears
The sobs in the dark, and the
dropping of tears."

Sometimes my tales were ludicrous scenes at the suppers given, and presided over by Mr. (now Sir) Walter Besant. She was very sympathetic with young people, and recognized the importance of trying to influence and direct

the minds of future genera-
tions.

She rallied considerably in
the spring of 1894, and wrote,
"Thank you for flowers, which
bring a country charm and
freshness to our world of
brick and mortar. Not that I
despise the Square trees, which
are greening delightfully.
Those wild blue hyacinths,
not to speak of their com-
panions, have a special hold
on me."

Of her last Easter on earth
she wrote, "Every blessing
of this blessed season to

you. Thank you for the pretty primroses and daisies in their envelope of moss. Thank you for wishing me well. I am not perhaps quite at my best, but I cannot now expect to reach a high standard of health and strength. I should like to have been able to place flowers on my own mother's grave at Easter, even as you placed some on yours, but my health forbids such a pleasure."

Shortly after she wrote, " The weather here is perfect,

and a box of primroses, etc.,
has come to-day, bringing
something of the country to
my little room; so I need
not envy you your prim-
roses! And now we are
having thunder since I wrote
that."

Two other letters I re-
ceived. The last, June 11,
1894, commences, " I am very
unwell."

Then came a card in July—
" Weak and ill, but glad to
hear from you.

" Always yours,

" C. G. Rossetti."

Another card in July, and
the last I received—

"Too ill for much writing,
but glad of news of you, and
sympathizing in what you tell
me.

"C. G. R."

She lived nearly five months
after this, but I only received
messages through the nurse,
such as "Miss Rossetti sends
you her dear love, and bids
me say she no longer reads or
writes her own letters." She
suffered a great deal at this
time, and her patience and

fortitude were beyond all praise. She prayed daily for all her friends, and thanked her nurse repeatedly for her kind offices, saying, " I cannot thank you enough, but my mother will thank you in heaven."

In December, 1894, I saw, from the tone of the bulletins I received, that the end was fast approaching, and left Ireland for London. I saw her on the 21st, but what a change ! The fine features sharpened by agony that was past. She lay on a couch in the drawing-room. When the nurse announced me, she unclosed her eyes with a look which said, "You see how weak I am; I cannot speak." In fact, she rarely spoke at this stage. Her brother watched constantly beside her couch, but during the last fortnight of her life she seldom spoke, even to him. She was mercifully spared much pain at this period. Again I saw her on December 23, her last Sunday on earth, but she slept. The doctor came almost at the same time, and would not disturb her. And very peaceful she looked, recalling her own lines—

" She sleeps a charmèd sleep:
    Awake her not.

.   .   .   .   .

Rest, rest, a perfect rest,
Shed over brow and breast ;
Her face is toward the west,
    The purple land."

My household cares called me back; I could only kneel beside her for a few minutes, and kiss her cold forehead. I then thought death was near; she lived, however, five days longer. During this time her lips were constantly moving in prayer, and on the morning of December 29 she passed quietly away.

"Her quiet eyelids closed; she had
   Another morn than ours."

She herself wrote—

" When flowers are yet in bud,
   While the boughs are green,
   I would get quit of earth,
   And get robed for heaven;
Putting on my raiment white within
      the screen,
Putting on my crown of gold whose
      gems are seven."

We can have no doubt the latter part of this wish was fulfilled. Of the former, she says—

" So spring must dawn again with
    warmth and bloom,
  Or in this world or in the world
    to come.
    Sing, voice of spring,
  Till I too blossom, and rejoice
    and sing."

And again—

" I wonder if the spring-tide of
    this year
  Will bring another spring both
    lost and dear ;
  If heart and spirit will find out
    their spring,
  Or if the world alone will bud
    and sing?
    Sing, Hope, to me ;
  Sweet notes, my Hope, soft notes
    for memory."

On the margin of this she

wrote, " I was walking in the outer circle, Regent's Park, when the impulse or thought came to me."

She has entered on her first heavenly spring, where flowers fairer than primroses or her beloved wild hyacinths meet her eyes. But more than all, the love she pined for, even the love of Christ that passeth knowledge, she can now comprehend with all saints. As she writes—

" Love that dost pass the tenfold
seven times seven,
Draw Thou mine eyes, draw Thou
my heart above ;

My treasure and my heart store
　　Thou in Thee."

If ever heart was drawn
above, hers was. The world
and the world's joys had no
place in it. Her great
humility was one of her chief
characteristics; never self-
asserting, but in lowliness of
mind considering others better
than herself. This great
humility she expresses in one
poem—

" Give me the lowest place : not
　　that I dare
　Ask for that lowest place, but
　　Thou hast died."

To those who knew her intimately, these words are known to be the expression of her continual thought. It was pain to her to be praised, or to hear any panegyric on her works. Not very long before her death, a paragraph was read to her from some paper, thinking it would interest her. Her comment was, "Woe unto you when all men praise you!"

It may be there were times when flesh and heart would fail; as she writes—

“ Alas for him
Who faints, despite thy Pattern, King
   of Saints !
Alas, alas, for me the one that
   faints !

.   .   .   .   .   .

But when our strength shall be
   made weakness, and our bodies
   clay,
Hold Thou us fast, and give us
   sleep till day.”

Her favourite text during her last illness, “ I will trust, and not be afraid,” was placed in such a position by her desire that her eyes might rest upon it at all times.

But, above all, her chief characteristic was love—love

to the whole human family. She never realized evil. Living such a retired life, more like a cloistered nun than anything else, she knew little of the world or its ways, and refused on principle to have any distrust. I don't think, in all her writings, one bitter or harsh expression can be found against any member of the human family. Hers was the charity that thinketh no evil. Her fervent piety and childlike faith appear as one of the green spots in a desert, amidst the doubt and despair to which our century has attained. Her memory will be much cherished in Christ Church, Woburn Square, where she was for many years a devout worshipper.

Her memorial sermon, by the incumbent, Rev. J. J. Nash, has been published, and gives details not mentioned here. She sleeps under no stately dome, but as she herself desired, when she wrote long ago—

" Be the green grass above me
  With showers and dewdrops
  wet.

" I shall not see the shadows,
    I shall not feel the rain ;
I shall not hear the nightingale
    Sing on, as if in pain :
And dreaming through the twilight
    That doth not rise nor set,
Haply I may remember,
    And haply may forget."